The Bohemians
Vol. 2

CARLOS L. ROSARIO GONZALEZ

Copyright © 2021 Carlos L. Rosario Gonzalez

All rights reserved.

ISBN: 9798717022828

To all the young souls who lost count of body counts and simply fell in love.

Rosario Gonzalez

CONTENTS

	Author's Note	7
1	Charlie | *The Girl from Portofino*	10
2	Freddy | *The Casino Script*	28
3	Maddy | *Best Friends in New York*	46
4	Blake | *Saying Adiós to Corazón*	52
5	John | *Merci*	70
6	… | *Machu Picchu*	86
7	Katelyn | *2020*	104
	Epilogue	113
	Acknowledgment	
	About the Author	

Author's Note

When I first wrote *The Bohemians* I didn't have an "endgame." Were these bohemians part of an interconnected literary universe that I still hadn't yet conceived? That idea came about after I published Volume One. I had already introduced a supernatural element with Freddy's chapter. And even in John's story—when he descended into alcoholic madness—an other-wordly vibe kind of crept into the overarching romantic theme. It was clear that the story was heading into the fantastical. However, I knew I didn't want these dudes to become superheroes. This was a "fish out of water" situation. These guys were to step into a very different type of world, while still yearning for that one thing that made them bohemians in the first place: love.

Obviously, while these stories read like a memoir, they aren't entirely true. Some carry more truths than others and are inspired by real-life events that transpired in the lives of the people who these characters are based off.

A lot has changed since the first volume. There are new characters who I hope you like as much as I loved putting them to the page. The character based on me (who I also just happened to name Carlos) is one interesting fellow. You still might think that all of these Bohemians are all the same person, but I promise that's not true. *Or is it?*

Thank you for reading.

"He knew that when he kissed this girl, and forever wed his unutterable visions to her perishable breath, his mind would never romp again like the mind of God."

- *The Great Gatsby*, F. Scott Fitzgerald

Ch. 1

Charlie

The Girl from Portofino

THE GIRL FROM PORTOFINO

The Bohemians

—

Drinking wine in Italy is a sport. Even with a big plate of pasta and bread, and two espresso cappuccinos *para il bambino*, as the baristas called me, I ended up wasted two hours into our Roman adventure. That's when John, with his excellent Italian, convinced the hotel clerks that we had booked a room for spring break. After unpacking, it wasn't long until we found a party. There, John met Dianna. However, he, like the rest of us, was drunk to the core and made a complete fool of himself.

The morning after, John even forced us to look for Dianna in a museum where he thought she'd be, but we couldn't find her. She had vanished. I didn't care. My girlfriend at the time, Brooke, texted me to ask whether I could pick up some things from her childhood home in Portofino, before my flight back to America. I agreed. The only issue was that it was a five-hour train ride from Rome. John and the rest of the Bohemians were still on the hunt for Dianna so I was to board the train by myself and find something to keep me busy. It's funny how the universe decides to spin things around.

You truly never get what you think is up ahead. On a train to Portofino, on an errand from my girlfriend, that's where I met Lucia.

I sat alone for an hour before I noticed a young woman staring at me from a few seats over. I was sitting next to the window and her reflection was all the proof I needed that this lady had her eyes on me. A few minutes later a waiter, who was also the conductor, passed by and stopped by my seat.

"*Salve, signore.* A cappuccino for you, from the lady over there." The waiter placed a cup on the table in front of me, then, after stamping my boarding ticket, turned around to serve another guest. The woman then stood and approached, sitting across from me. Her red lipstick, a shade right out of some 1970s erotic thriller, demanded my attention. I wondered how many men (or women) she had kissed; I wanted to be all of them. It was a thought that happened in an instant, like an automated response, that it took some time for me to realize that the idea of cheating on Brooke had already entered my subconscious.

"Hi, my name is Lucia," she said with a heavy Italian accent. "Lucia Visconti."

"Thank you for the coffee, Lucia," I said, now moved by the greenish tint of her eyes. Hypnotic they were, like Cleopatra's. The same ones that made Mark Anthony kneel down with affection. And, without question, those same eyes from Elizabeth Taylor that destroyed the on-screen Republic, and bankrupted a film studio in real life. I kept my wallet in close watch.

"Excuse me if this is a little… strange, but I wanted to introduce myself," Lucia said. "It's the Italian way."

"Oh no, I'm quite aware. You've been looking at me for a while now," I said. I tapped my window. "Your reflection ratted you out."

Lucia laughed. "You are very funny. What is your name?"

"Charlie." It felt so plain compared to hers. So unromantic.

"There's not many people on this train, Mr. Charlie. I hope you don't mind if I start a conversation," she said.

"Not at all. There's only so much you can do on your phone before boredom takes over. And we've got four more hours to go." It was definitely the Italian way because such a scene would've never happened in the States. The roles would likely be reversed, but even then, a stranger approaching a lone woman in America has sinister connotations. Apparently, it was different in Italy, and I believed it. Brooke had that same forward proactiveness.

"So, where are you heading?" I said.

"To Portofino. It's a beautiful place."

"Really? Want to take a guess at my destination?"

She smiled. "Well, it doesn't surprise me. You said it yourself, we've got four hours to go." She then laughed.

"What is it?" I said, intrigued, and now careful as to not reveal much more. Regardless of Lucia's beauty, she was still a stranger.

"You are not a tourist. At least not at the moment. Tourists travel in groups. You are alone… A handsome, young man on his way to Portofino, all by himself. *That is interesting.*" Her tone grew more flirtatious. "What brings you to Portofino, mister Charlie?"

It felt as though Lucia was deliberately steering the conversation in a specific direction, yet a torrent of haphazard words kept spilling out of my mouth. She deduced me so well. Her red lips kept staring at me. Her green eyes as well. Her voice enchanting me; accent and all, an Italian incantation. Soon, my mind began to wander, as I imagined kissing her... I stopped myself and shook my head.

"I'm picking up some things in Portofino," I said. "For my girlfriend." I had to mention Brooke. To stop anything before it started.

"Oh, you have a girlfriend?" Lucia said. "I'm not surprised... What's her name?"

"Brooke. She's Italian . . . like you. From Portofino." I was telling a stranger everything about my life while I knew nothing about hers; I tried to think of a question to ask, but I soon began to feel dizzy. "Trains, you know, they make me..." And I fell asleep.

The conductor was the face I saw when I opened my eyes. "*Signore?*"

"Oh, hey. What... time is it?" I said.

"Time to wake up. We've arrived at your destination."

I'd been asleep for four hours. The last thing I remembered was Lucia. Her name tattooed to my mind, plus all of her features. *Lucia Visconti*. I then checked my back pocket. My wallet was still there. I checked inside. My money, passport card; all there. Nothing was missing. I then checked my side pockets. My phone was still there. I then checked if any mysterious messages were sent to Brooke, or the Bohemians, or if any nasty social media posts were made, but everything was just as it was. I was relieved, but still, very much confused.

"Can I see your boarding pass, signore," said the conductor.

I couldn't find it. Of all things, *that* was missing.

"I… can't seem to find it," I said. "Why do you need it?"

He looked at me, concerned. "*Signore*, you understand that without that boarding pass you won't be able to board this train back to Rome tomorrow? Your ticket was the only one marked round trip. It is my duty to remind our guests."

I had bought my ticket at the station, so I didn't have a digital version that I could access from my phone. I'd also forgotten to snap a picture of it. All seemed lost.

I checked all over my seat and couldn't find anything. "I'll buy another one," I told the conductor.

"I'm afraid this train is the only one leaving for Rome tomorrow from Portofino. It's sold out, *signore*. After tomorrow however, on Monday night, there's still availability."

"I'll figure it out," I told him. Leaving on Monday for Rome was out of the question. My return flight home was that Monday morning. Before I stepped off the train I asked him one last thing.

"Do you remember that woman who bought me the cappuccino? Do you know which way she went? I'm new here in town."

"*Si*. Toward the docks... Thank you for reminding me." He handed me what appeared to be a restaurant menu. "She wanted me to give you..."

"What am I supposed to do with this?" I asked.

"*Signore*, I don't know what to tell you."

He was as confused as I was. I thanked him and tipped him. There I was in Portofino, without a return ticket home and with a random restaurant menu in my hand. Below the word PORTOFINO in big red letters, the menu only had three items: an appetizer (*Olive al Sugo*), an entrée (*Le Migliori Fettucine*), and dessert (*Il Tiramisù Classico*). *No drinks?* I wondered.

I was so fixated on this menu (and with everything that had transpired on the train) that at first I failed to appreciate the magnificence of Portofino. It felt more relaxed than Rome; the streets were narrower, the bricks and stones more vibrant, and the tightly-stacked village homes more colorful. Cuba, but Italian. An Ernest Hemingway identity. I headed down towards the docks where Lucia had apparently gone. All I could find were big, expensive boats hauling piles of fish as far as the eye could see. If *The Old Man and the Sea* had been set here, Santiago would've beaten his unlucky streak months in advance.

I wasn't hungry, but the menu kept teasing me. I looked for a restaurant called PORTOFINO. That was all I cared about now. Yes, I knew that I had to pick up Brooke's things, but I couldn't return to Rome with them unless I tracked down Lucia first. My only clue was that menu. However, unlike most folks in Rome, few people knew English in Portofino. Directions and clarity soon became a rare commodity.

"Do you know if there is a restaurant called PORTOFINO around here?" I asked an older couple.

"There are many restaurants in Portofino, *amico*," said the husband.

I was getting nowhere.

Then, as one of the big yachts started to undock, I caught a glimpse of its name: PORTOFINO. *Perhaps the menu isn't for a restaurant after all.* The thought raced through my mind.

I ran as fast as I could toward the yacht, waving my hands like a crazy person. I was too late. The yacht was gone. I took my phone out and used the camera as "binoculars," zooming in to see if I could find Lucia among the many women in swimsuits chilling on the deck. It seemed like they were having a good time. Alas, I couldn't find her. Then, I heard a voice. There was someone behind me.

"Good luck getting on that boat, *amico*." It was…

"Lucia," I said.

"Visconti? My sister? You know her . . . ?" Apparently, Lucia had a sibling. A *twin* sibling.

"You are fucking with me, right?"

"No. My name is Gianna, Gianna Visconti. Lucia is on that boat."

I still couldn't believe it. "Well, your sister stole my boarding ticket back to Rome. I need it back."

Gianna smiled. "Yeah, that's something she would do." She paused. "Okay, I'll help you."

"You don't even know me. Why help a stranger?" I said.

"Because I also want to get on that boat."

Her voice had the exact same intonation as Lucia's, but Gianna's face had a subtle difference; she had a cute mole above her lip on the left side of her mouth like the singer INNA's.

"Alright. Why would your sister steal my boarding pass?" I said.

"One of Lucia's girlfriends is having a party in Rome tomorrow," Gianna said. "Maybe she ran out of money for her own ticket?" She then showed me the inside of her purse. No cash, just nail polish and other beauty utensils; no red lipstick. "You are not the only victim of my thief of a sister."

"So, um, how are we getting on that boat?" I said.

"Follow me."

I didn't hesitate. Gianna had the same insuppressible magnetism as her sister. She took me up a hill where, from the terrace garden of a hotel where I could never afford a night's stay, we could see all of Portofino . . . and the big yacht in the distance.

"This is the Cervara Abbey. Beautiful, isn't it?" Gianna said. "There's the boat. It won't go too far out into the sea."

"It'll be back?" I said.

"Yeah. It's only a matter of when. Probably midnight, or later."

"No, no, no. I don't have that kind of time. I thought you said you wanted to get on that boat."

She smiled. "The PORTOFINO is the biggest yacht in the village. They have a party every night, off the coast, in the middle of the sea. The *best* parties. If you pick the right night, you might even catch a celebrity. The hard part is getting in. But you already have that covered."

"The menu. That's how you get in?"

"Yeah," she said. "The menus get shredded as soon as you enter the boat. There's actually no food served on the PORTOFINO. Only drinks and… some other things."

"You seem to know a lot about this boat. I get it now. In exchange for getting my train pass back, you want the yacht menu."

She nodded. "*Sì.*"

"Okay, Gianna. Look, I'm not waiting until nightfall for this boat to return. If we've got until midnight, then I need to do something. You can follow *me* now."

I followed my Google Maps route to Brooke's old childhood home. Brooke had told me that the key would be under a miniature statue of Aphrodite next to the door. It was.

"What are we looking for?" asked Gianna.

"A red cassette and a fancy rosary. It's silver, with a ruby on the cross, instead of Lord Almighty."

As we looked around, the dusty family photos of Brooke made me smile.

"She is a lucky girl to have you," said Gianna, locking eyes with me.

"I don't deserve her," I said, looking away. And I meant it. I had never cheated on Brooke, yet I still felt guilty for my thoughts about Lucia back on the train. And for my thoughts about Gianna at that very moment. I was hooked.

"Why would you say that?" Gianna said, grabbing my hand.

"Because I've been having . . . y'know . . . thoughts."

Gianna then said the strangest of things. "My *witch* of a sister. She probably poisoned you with her love potion."

"The cappuccino…" I said. "Must've knocked me

out."

"I'm sorry," she said, as though she felt guilt by association.

I snapped out of it. "My feelings for *you* are not the works of some caffeinated elixir, Gianna." Then I came to a realization. "Why haven't you asked for my name?"

Gianna locked eyes with me. "I fear if I get to know you, I might fall for you...." She paused. "You do not want *me*. You want my sister... I, I..."

We kissed. Gianna took her top off and pressed against me so hard that I stumbled back into a nightstand; its cabinet opened, revealing Brooke's cassette and silver rosary.

"Wait." I looked down. "There it is."

We came to our senses shortly after. Gianna put her top back on.

"What's the cassette?" Gianna asked. "A mixtape?"

"I don't know," I said. "We . . . shouldn't have done that."

I slid to the floor, disappointed in myself for succumbing to temptation. Gianna sat beside me, our backs to the wall.

"Look, we can talk about it," she said. "Unlike my

sister, I have a heart."

"There's nothing to be said. I cheated on Brooke. With you."

"You clearly like her. You are here in Portofino. That's obvious. What you did was a choice. *Why* did you make that choice?" Gianna was serious.

"What *we* did."

"No," she said. "I did what I did for my own reasons. Why did *you*?

She had a point. It took me a minute to understand. "You tell me first."

"It's not every day that I get to meet a handsome American." She chuckled. "Like getting on that boat, I don't know when there will be a next time. This is Portofino. If you're lucky, you might see a celebrity. I've got to enjoy my luck while it lasts."

"Whoa," I said, truly amazed.

"Whoa," she said back, with a smirk.

We smiled.

"Your turn, *amico*."

"Brooke is what you might call my first real girlfriend. Unlike my friends, I'm not very good at the hookup thing. You know what that phrase means, right?"

Gianna nodded.

"There was never anyone before Brooke," I continued. "At all. When it comes to love, sex, all that stuff, she has taught me everything. The Bohemians say I lucked out with Brooke…"

"The Bohemians?" Gianna said, confused.

"Sorry, that's what John calls us . . . my friends." I waved the subject away. "Look, Brooke is gorgeous. She looks like a fucking supermodel. She's high-class, but very much unlike the stereotype. She's nice, sincere, and the smartest person I know. She's going to graduate with the highest honors. She's perfect. We've been together since junior year…"

Gianna then, again, grabbed my hand. "You can say it now."

"However, there's a lot more I want to experience. That's why I made my choice. I don't want to feel left out."

She then let go and stood back up. She offered her hand and I too stood up from the floor.

"You know, cheating on her here, in her home, it's almost like she gave you permission," Gianna said. "You are going to be all right. Tell her what happened. It's going to be okay."

"That's… an odd thing to say," I said, startled.

We both laughed.

"Come on, not close to midnight yet, but we can have pasta by the docks while we wait for the boat."

I smiled. "I like the sound of that."

As we walked out the door, "What is your name, *amico?*"

I laughed. "Finally. It's Charlie."

It was midnight now. As we waited for our order, Gianna was munching on some sweet olives. I couldn't help but notice its resemblance to the menu's appetizer. Our pasta then arrived.

"At last," said Gianna. "This is the best fettuccini in Portofino."

Again, my mind went to the menu. *The word **best** in Italian is **Miglore**… Il Miglore Fettuccini; the entree…*

I couldn't quite put the pieces together. Then…

"Mr. Charlie, look at me." She took the nail polish bottle and a cotton swab out of her purse, and after dabbing the swab in the alcohol, she followed to disintegrate the mole by her mouth. It was fake.

"Lucia? What's going on?" I said, in utter surprise.

"Here's your boarding pass back to Rome. Cousin Brooke wanted to surprise you. She knows how you've been feeling, lately."

"This was all her idea… Wait, you mean… We could've done more?"

She laughed. "Don't push it. Brooke's still your girlfriend." She laughed again as she shook her head. "Welcome to Portofino, Charlie. Welcome to the Family."

"Wow. 'The Italian way,' huh?"

"You know, you are not the drunk bastard I thought you were going to be," Gianna said. "Good kisser too. Cuz taught you well."

With a smile, I shook my head. "That's 'cause you've only spent one day with me." I then laughed. "Now when's the tiramisu coming?"

Ch. 2

Freddy

The Casino Script

The Bohemians

—

When Freddy was a little boy, he always dreamed of becoming a movie star. He grew up with two sisters—one served as captain of their high school cheerleading team while the other eventually signed with a modeling agency. It was obvious his sisters' popular lifestyle influenced the young Frederick, as grade after grade, his affinity for women was fine-tuned to rich white blondes. His sisters' friends conquered his space one slumber party at a time. When college came around, he already had a type.

Nurtured to having such particular likings soon proved to be a curse for Freddy. While he prized every sorority invitation he received, he despised how easy such a feat was to attain. There were many frat boys who could only wish to attend at least one of the many extravagant parties from those Sigma houses, yet Freddy had the golden ticket. Even though he had his eyes, and his heart, locked on a single woman—a girl named Maddy—Freddy looked forward to meeting the type of pretty girls who many years ago invaded his childhood home. Thanks to his sisters, he knew exactly what to say to get what he wanted, and exactly how and when to say it. This proved particularly useful when Freddy graduated from college and transitioned into his first job, as a writer's assistant for an indie film distribution company in New York called Venus Trap. His new boss was a smart, young woman named Katelyn, and like his sisters and their friends, she embodied that same opulent archetype that Freddy grew to adore.

"We've just acquired our next big hit. It's in pre-production right now but I think it's going to be marvelous," Katelyn told Freddy, now six months on the job.

He had been doing tremendous work since the first day that Katelyn saw in Freddy a trustworthy confidant. No one below the executive level was supposed to know of Venus Trap's latest acquisition, but it was important for Katelyn to keep Freddy in the loop. Her main responsibilities required her to rewrite any part of the film's script that needed an overhaul. Since she also served as a marketing executive for the company, she delegated the majority of the writing projects to Freddy.

"Spit it out, Kate. What's the movie about? When does shooting start?" asked Freddy.

Katelyn smiled. "Slow down. I'm getting to that. Of course, there's going to be some rewrites. You'll be tackling that. It's a gambling movie, with some supernatural elements. Think *Casino* meets *The Exorcist*. Shooting starts in one month so I'll need those rewrites ASAP."

Freddy had never written anything pertaining to gambling or casinos. However, his college days consisted of sorority parties and poker nights at his dorm. This was a subject he knew all too well. "This should be fun. Another question, though… You know I've always wanted to visit a movie set… Can I come?"

Katelyn knew sooner or later that Freddy would ask such a question. "I wish it was up to me, Freddy."

He smiled, accepting defeat. "Thought I'd ask."

Even though Freddy aspired to one day become the next Leonardo DiCaprio, he had other reasons why he wanted to attend the film's production: Katelyn was going to be there. It only took about two months for Freddy to think of his boss in a new light. Already six months in and his fantasies were spiraling out of control. In his breaks at work, he would write about Katelyn, making her the main character in a series of poems about love and conquest. Perhaps it was the proximity, or the day-to-day constant communication with Katelyn that made him think of her as he did Maddy. A day or two was the most Freddy had spent with his sorority hookups, and while Maddy was the outlier that succeeded in snatching his heart, Katelyn had all the attributes that he desired. Even more, she was a challenge. Indeed, Katelyn already had a boyfriend.

Freddy didn't know the scope of Katelyn's relationship. She rarely mentioned her boyfriend at work. Not even his name. All Freddy knew was that he lived in Jersey. *How do you conquer a woman's heart when you don't even know your enemy?* Freddy was careful not to raise such a subject. He and Katelyn were close, but that was a boundary he still hadn't tested and one that came with high risk. Seeking romance at the risk of losing a good job was not in Freddy's plans, but if the logline of his love life was ever to be written, he needed to uncover the secrets of his boss' heart, one way or the other. Freddy found the perfect excuse when he finally finished the casino script two weeks in advance.

"That was quick!" Katelyn said. "Thanks. I'll read it

tonight and have some notes for you tomorrow morning."

"I think you'll like it. The only issue I was having was with the romantic relationship between the main characters. It's the long-distance aspect of it. I tried my best, but I don't think it's believable." Freddy hoped the comment would trigger a response from Katelyn. It was a wild assumption to make based on the fact that her boyfriend *supposedly* lived in New Jersey. Katelyn could've been lying. Or, perhaps her boyfriend lived in Hoboken, or Fort Lee, both a mere 25-minute drive (on a good day) from Manhattan. It was a longshot.

"Hmmm…" She said. "Experience *is* the best source."

"What was that?" Freddy said, blood racing.

His assumptions were correct. Yet, he didn't expect what came next.

"I changed my mind. I'll read it over later today. What's your schedule looking like for seven tonight?"

"I'm good. What's happening at seven?" Freddy said, anxiously waiting for her next words.

"You like sushi? We'll dine and talk notes. I may have some pointers for you."

I'm going on a date with my boss? To talk about her boyfriend? Freddy's poetic mind just flew.

Katelyn continued. "And don't worry. It's going on the company card. Venus has us covered."

That night, Freddy arrived early to the restaurant. A waiter walked him to his table.

Katelyn arrived not long after. "Early bird like me, I see."

Freddy laughed. "I went ahead and ordered some starters. Edamame. That's all right?"

"That's perfect. I'm starving."

"So how was your day?" Freddy said, trying to make small talk.

She laughed. "That's so corny, Freddy. Try again."

"What?" said Freddy, holding a laugh. He knew he now had an opening, but still, he treaded lightly. "Ahhh… I knew it, so this is a date. I promise I'm not like the other dudes. Pinky-promise."

Katelyn laughed. "Not bad, not bad. I had a feeling you were one of those kids in college."

"Who are *those*?" Freddy asked, now intrigued.

"Like those smooth-talkers from college. I'm not that much older than you, Freddy. I know your type.

Suave like that." She laughed again. "I hope you didn't break any girls' hearts."

Freddy giggled. "I mean…"

"Freddy! Nooo… You are a heartbreaker?"

"It's not my fault. That's college. We are just having fun. Sometimes the other person catches feelings and you don't. Hookups. You know what I'm talking about."

Katelyn took a long look at Freddy, which made him nervous. *Did I go too far?* His mind kept running in circles. But then, she smirked.

"I guess I might've broken some poor boys' hearts."

Freddy made a go for it. "See, you are just like me. Your boyfriend is one of the lucky ones that got away."

"If only we had met in college. I wouldn't have had to deal with all those bad breakups."

Freddy asked away, not losing momentum. "Oh, where'd you guys meet?"

"It's a long story. Think the opening scene of *Meet Joe Black*, before Brad Pitt goes to heaven. Lloyd was so suave, like you. Knew exactly what to say."

There it was. Freddy had done it. His opponent finally had a name. By now both had already ordered sushi, but their plates were a long way from being empty. Freddy was purposely eating slowly, but even Katelyn seemed to have slowed down her pace despite her hunger.

"Speaking of Lloyd," Katelyn said. "Your rewrite, as always, fantastic. You can improve on the long-distance relationship, though. You could learn a thing or two about my situation. You see, Lloyd lives in Atlanta now. I've had to get used to this long-distance thing myself."

"Oh, I didn't know. How is that, exactly?" Freddy said.

"It's complicated. There's a lot to unpack and one date night won't cut it."

"A second date? Aren't you moving a little too fast, Katelyn?" Freddy was now loose.

Katelyn laughed. "Even better." She took out a small rectangular piece of paper from her purse. "You've always wanted to visit a movie set, right?"

Freddy couldn't believe it. "No fucking way!" It was a plane ticket.

"We're off to L.A. in a couple days. Start packing, we're going to be spending a lot of time together."

Freddy and Katelyn flew to Los Angeles on a Friday night and arrived at LAX the following morning on

Saturday. Freddy, now seemingly closer with his boss, decided to play it safe and avoid any conversation about Lloyd during the flight. Instead, they only talked about the movie.

"Marlon Marcus Paul was just announced as the main lead," said Katelyn.

Freddy, surprised, said, "Really? Wasn't he rumored to be in that new MCU movie?"

"Yeah. He passed on it to be in our project."

"Our indie film over the role of a lifetime?" said Freddy. "Wow."

Katelyn smiled. "I heard he only said yes after he read your rewrite. See, Freddy. Your words are persuasive; powerful. Don't get too excited, though. We still got work to do on the relationship aspect. That part of the script won't start shooting 'til next week."

After landing in Los Angeles, Freddy and Katelyn took an Uber to their hotel. Venus Trap booked two separate rooms for the two employees, floors apart. And, while their chemistry was growing the more they spent time with each other, for Freddy, sleeping with his boss never came to mind. Unlike with his first love Maddy, sex was insignificant this time around. For

Freddy, conquering Katelyn's heart was the mission. Only one person stood in his way. Lloyd became the subject of conversation later that night at dinner.

"Okay, Freddy. Long-distance relationships are hard. In a way, they are a self-fulfilling prophecy."

"How so?" said Freddy. "That's not a good thing, right?"

"I trust Lloyd. He trusts me. But he's a man."

They both laughed.

Katelyn continued. "I just hope he doesn't make a mistake in Atlanta… with somebody else."

"Why would thinking that cause it to happen? Like, I get the gist, but—"

"You are a smartass, you know." Katelyn just smiled.

"Boss, I'm just saying if there's trust between the two of you, then there's nothing to worry about."

Freddy then donned a curious expression.

"What is it?" asked Katelyn.

"Can I ask you a question? It's about Lloyd. I swear it's for the script."

"What else would it be for?" She laughed. "What's up?"

"Those thoughts. Do *you* ever think of making a mistake with somebody else?"

◆◆◆

"Hmmm…" Katelyn pondered. Perhaps the thought had floated through her mind one time she saw a cute athletic guy running with his dog on the Brooklyn Bridge. That it was Freddy asking the question, opened the gates to other more specific questions in her head. *Have I ever thought of Freddy like I think Lloyd?*

Katelyn had boundaries. She was a professional and like Freddy, knew to keep compliments strictly work-related. However, she knew that she and Freddy were the "hottest" duo working on the Venus Trap writing department, and certain looks carry certain assumptions. It didn't bother her once when a fellow executive asked her if she was having a fling with her subordinate. Katelyn derided the idea, but ever since that day, those kinds of thoughts kept clinging to her mind. Yet, it was less if she would ever start an affair with Freddy, and more if Freddy ever had such wild thoughts about her. Now, it seemed that Katelyn was testing her hypothesis.

◆◆◆

"Freddy, I don't want you to feel like you are in an uncomfortable position. But I've noticed a pattern in you that's eerily reminiscent of a past experience. I'm going to answer your question with a question. Is that okay?"

Freddy nodded with butterflies in his stomach.

Katelyn continued. "You know, I met Lloyd while working as an intern at *Vanity Fair*. He was an editorial assistant for *The New Yorker*, up a floor. We met in the elevator, on our way up. Our hands touched when we went for our floor's buttons. He would come down to have lunch with me every day until I was offered your job at Venus Trap. After I got promoted, he then applied for your position, to be closer to me. He was hired, but didn't last long. His dreams took him to Atlanta. He… wants to be a famous rapper. What is *your* dream?"

Freddy had a dilemma. He wasn't sure if they were still talking about the script. He had insinuated an affair with Katelyn, but perhaps this "dream" question was her attempt at redirecting the conversation. In his mind, he had two options. One; confess his lover boy dreams, with hopes that Katelyn's situation with Lloyd was as complicated as it seemed. It was risky, but the window was now wide open to put everything on the table with minimal blowback. *Surely, she would understand?* Option two was just as critical; keep it professional and commit to his Hollywood dreams. He would be meeting Marlon Marcus Paul very soon. *With a contact like him, anything can happen.* He rolled the dice. This was a religious gamble he was willing to take.

"Let's keep the game rolling for just a bit longer," said Freddy. "I'm going to answer your answer to my question with a question of my own."

"Go on," said Katelyn, now more intrigued than ever.

"Did you ask this same question to *Lloyd* before he left for Atlanta?"

◆◆◆

The question caught Katelyn by surprise. Freddy was good with words, but this strategic chess move—as she saw it—piqued her interest. He had caught on to her implications, unlike those boys from her past, yet ironically, just like Lloyd. To her, though, it was funny that this particular circumstance would happen outside of New York. Like Freddy, she would always tread lightly on subjects deemed taboo for the workplace. But now, all was fair game and her curiosity was coming to a head. Honesty was her most valuable weapon.

◆ ◆ ◆

"Yes," said Katelyn, with a poker face Freddy hadn't seen since his worst cash games in college. She was unreadable.

Yet, this didn't matter for Freddy. A bluff or not, in that particular instance, it was insignificant. *Checkmate.*

"What is your dream, Freddy?"

"My dream is to live a life without regrets. That's... a life where I wake up in the morning and the first thing I see is the smile on your face."

Katelyn looked down, blushing. *Did he just...* She then looked at Freddy. "It's going to be a long day tomorrow. We should call it a night."

That night, Freddy went up to his room with a weight off his shoulders. Regardless of what came next, he had delivered his confession in the best of circumstances. Katelyn, however, now knew that her most loyal employee was also in love with her. For once in her life, she hated to be right. Still, she faced an even greater realization. Freddy had chosen her, unlike her boyfriend Lloyd. She contemplated all the ways that their work relationship would change. *A self-fulfilling prophecy.* She thought that night of going down to Freddy's room and "let the universe handle the rest," but to her surprise, she was the one who heard a knock on her door.

"I'm sorry, Katelyn. It was very inappropriate of me to say those things. But you were honest with me and I wanted to be honest with you. You will have my resignation letter tomorrow morning."

Katelyn shook her head. "Not going to happen. I'm not losing my best employee because of *feelings*. You've got some serious balls, though. I'll give you that."

Freddy smiled, then with a soft tone, "I'm guessing we can never be together then?"

"We can work together. We just can't be together," Katelyn said. Then, for reassurance, "Are you really in love with me Freddy? Or is it something *else* you want?"

There was no poker face or misdirection. Freddy understood. "Don't take it the wrong way, but no, I don't want to have sex with you."

Katelyn laughed. "For God's sake, Freddy. 'To fuck.' No one says 'to have sex with you.'"

"I didn't want to overstep," Freddy said, with a smile.

"Oh, we are way past that."

She then invited him in. Overlooking the L.A. city skyline, they lit a joint and opened a tiny bottle of Jim Beam from the mini fridge. Freddy's poems began to come to life.

"Just to be clear, I wasn't kidding about my dream. Did he really leave you like that? Lloyd."

"That's Lloyd Jenkins for you," said Katelyn.

"I still have my Hollywood dreams," said Freddy.

"I thought *I* was your dream."

Freddy took a sip of his drink and after a smile, said, "They are one and the same."

Katelyn laughed. "I don't get it."

"You really don't?"

She nodded.

"Well, I'm here in Hollywood, aren't I?"

Katelyn couldn't stop blushing. "Goddammit, Freddy. You and your fucking words." She then felt the urge to kiss him, but Freddy beat her to it.

"Goodnight, boss."

As he left and headed toward the elevator, Katelyn's mind traveled back to the past.

"Lloyd, I understand it's your dream. I have dreams too. But New York has all the same opportunities as Atlanta. All the labels are here."

"Babe, just imagine you and me running our own label. Your marketing skills with my artistic prowess. That's an incredible combo. I'm asking you to trust me."

"Lloyd… You are asking me to leave everything behind. Move to Atlanta. Start over…"

"It's what's best. Come with me, please…"

Then, as Freddy reached for his room's floor button on the elevator, Katelyn pressed DOOR CLOSE.

"Fuck Lloyd Jenkins." Katelyn plunged her body atop Freddy's, the sudden embrace taking them down to the ground.

They laughed.

Ch. 3

Maddy

Best Friends in New York

BEST FRIENDS IN NEW YORK

—

Freddy seldom visited Central Park. Though it wasn't far from Venus Trap, a mere two miles, he wasn't a "nature boy." A few days after he returned from Los Angeles, however, he and Maddy decided to catch up. They met at the park. For the first time ever, Freddy felt an urgent sensation to watch the leaves swing through the sky. His inner Ralph Waldo Emerson cried to him.

"I miss this, Freddy," said Maddy. "When was the last time we walked the park?"

"Not long after graduation. Almost right after we both moved to the City," said Freddy. "Yeah, it's been a while."

After walking for a minute, they sat by a nearby bench, up a slight hill, overlooking the massive New York City skyscrapers. They watched as a series of couples walked by.

"Remember when you and I had a thing? Back in college," said Maddy.

"How could I forget?" said Freddy, with a laugh. "You were my first."

Maddy smiled, "What a crazy trip that was."

"You mean all your naked roommates who just so happened to have other-worldly psychedelic drugs? Yeah, I'm surprised I still remember anything."

Maddy shook her head, with a grin. "You were mad 'cause they didn't join us."

"Well, obviously. College orgies don't happen every day."

"Oh Freddy, you never change. What's on your mind?"

Freddy took a deep breath. "I kind of did something with my boss."

"You had sex with your boss?"

"No!"

"Then what?" said Maddy. "When you say 'I did something with my boss,' the implication is pretty clear."

"We had a moment. Back in L.A. It was brief but I'd never felt such a rush before. Like I wanted to leave it all behind and be with her. Go with her to wherever. It's not even about sex. It's weird, I don't know. Maybe I kind of…"

"Fell in love with her?" said Maddy. "You never felt

like that with me?"

"Of course I did. Always. All those times. But this is different, Maddy. I don't know how else to explain it. And you are the only one I trust. The only one that understands me. I don't know what to do and I need your help."

Maddy looked up to the sky. Almost as if shouting, "Aaaah, Freddy!" She then looked straight at him. Relaxed. "You've changed."

"I'm stuck. Do I risk it all for her?" said Freddy, now holding Maddy's hand.

"You know that movie *When Harry Met Sally*?" asked Maddy.

Freddy nodded.

"The famous quote by Billy Crystal how a man and a woman can't be friends 'cause fucking gets in the way…"

"Sure," said Freddy. "What about it?"

"It's weird how that never manifested between us. We had sex, plenty, and still continued being good friends... In the movie, Harry and Sally ended up together."

Freddy, confused, "I don't see how this has anything

to do with me and Katelyn. What are you trying to say, Maddy?"

"That I miss Frat Boy Freddy."

Not since their first time in bed on that cold Halloween night had Maddy called him Frat Boy Freddy. She never saw Freddy as he saw her, but as time went on and the two messed around on drunk New York nights, crashing in each other's apartments after deep conversations at the bar, Maddy's heart succumbed to Fredy's touch. But it wasn't just physical. She had fallen in love.

"Maddy, are you being serious?" asked Freddy, quite amazed. "You were the one who told me all those years ago to indulge in the fun and ignore the rest."

"I guess seeing you have these feelings for somebody else makes me a bit jealous."

They both laughed, still holding hands.

"Maddy, I don't know. This is how I feel now. I really, really like Katelyn. I love you, but not like that."

Maddy sighed. "I guess that's karma, right? You were all over me and I looked the other way. Now the tables have turned."

A moment passed. "Speaking of movies, you know

what this reminds me of?" said Freddy. "Julia Roberts... *My Best Friend's Wedding.*"

Maddy laughed. "Don't worry, I won't sabotage your love life."

"Well, there needs to be one in order for you to even try," said Freddy, joining in her laughter. "Maddy, I don't know what to do. I could lose it all. Job, career... It's all on the line."

"Not everything. Just tell her how you feel and your intentions. Whatever happens... You've still got me."

Ch. 4

Blake

Saying Adiós to Corazón

SAYING ADIÓS TO CORAZÓN

The Bohemians

—

"All we've got is time." Those were the last words I said to Corazón. It riddles me why I strived so hard to make her like me, but at times I just think that I was pulling closer to lunacy. Was I craving love? To be loved? Is that *crazy*? Was I crazy for having feelings for a woman who didn't feel the same way? My infatuation for Corazón stemmed from our long friendship since our college days and the many broken hearts that I endured throughout all of hook-up culture. She seemed to be the only person who appreciated me for being me and despite my often antisocial tendencies, her manic persona kind of canceled out, or rather perfectly balanced out our opposite dispositions.

I looked up to Corazón. I wanted to be more than just friends and, on many occasions, I told her my intentions. "Blake, the Boyfriend," that's what I wanted to be. She would always laugh at the idea, but not in any mean-spirited way. She knew how much I liked her. I was very clear about that. Yet, after I accepted that we were never going to be together no matter how much I tried to make her fall in love with me, my feelings for her never left. Perhaps that's why she always stuck with me even after our days in college. Even after all those rejections, she never stopped being my friend. We'd hang out from time to time. We'd talk on the phone, text almost every day, and like we did back in college, hit up an ice cream shop or an amusement park to reminisce on the past. I always got excited when Corazón and I would meet, and though I was expecting that day where we would eventually part ways, it never occurred to me that it would happen in Casablanca.

Imagine my face when "Casablanca" was the word that came out of her mouth. The film nerd within me peaked, as if I was channeling Humphrey Bogart himself. *Corazón wants to go to Casablanca! With me!* We didn't fly alone, though. Grace, her best friend, and Grace's boyfriend, the ostentatious James Calhoun, were coming along. Grace won four plane tickets to Casablanca after participating in a social media giveaway. She obviously chose her boyfriend and best friend for the trip, but I was surprised when Corazón called me with the proposition. If Grace was her female best friend, then I must've been the male counterpart.

I met Grace back in college one time I visited Corazón's dorm. That's also where I met James. He brought his Playstation to the dorm while Corazón and Grace studied for a Marketing test. I'd already taken the test a week before and was there to pick out which questions on their study guide would be on the exam. Granted, not one exam in college is the same but my love for Corazón exceeded any good reason to point out the obvious. Time with her was essential. But James was a pest. He wouldn't shut his mouth when we were trying to study and whenever his game would freeze, his complaints became like chants at a football game. He even tried to belittle me for not joining him in his game and we almost got into a fight when he called me a pussy for helping out his girlfriend. We started calling each other names, loudly. I remember he even threw the controller at me. In mid-air I smacked it back and it hit him on the shoulder. If it wasn't for Corazón there would've been blood on her dorm carpet; his blood.

Luckily, James and Grace sat very far from my seat and Corazón's. The flight to Morocco was pleasant, even more when Corazón put her head on my shoulder, sleeping through the flight 'til we landed in Casablanca.

This was my first time visiting Africa and as soon as we stepped off the plane our faces seemed to melt from the heat. This was a different kind of hot. It was nothing like the tropical weather of the Caribbean or the pleasant humidity of the Florida Keys. Morocco's air was sharp, but mostly from the sand. Indeed, it was everywhere and I loved all of it. Merchants roamed the streets like in the movies. Street dancers performed mere feet away from us, almost like in that famous scene in Marrakesh from *The Man Who Knew Too Much*. Like Doris Day in that movie, Corazón was magnetic. Her blonde hair radiated in conjunction with the sun. That, I very much told her, and she only laughed. She was used to the many compliments I'd given her, but that instance in Casablanca, not even my monochromatic-imagined vision could ignore her golden vibes. The vibes were so strong that I even tried my semi-decent Mid-Atlantic accent, the likes of Bogart himself, on a couple of those antiquated compliments. Again, she only laughed. I was all for it.

We took a bus to our hotel in the middle of the city. We each stayed in separate rooms, except for Grace and James. James kept messing around with me, teasing me that Corazón was going to sleep all by herself; that I should've roomed with her. Of course, that wasn't a choice deemed for me. Never in the planning of the trip did Corazón bring up such a question, so I just didn't think about it. Though, in his efforts to annoy me, James succeeded. I couldn't help but think… *What if she did want to room with me after all? There must be a higher reason why she wanted me to come along?* James was good at putting thoughts inside my head. Especially when it pertained to Corazón. That night during dinner at a local restaurant, while James and Grace were busy dancing on the floor, I spoke with Corazón to finally clear my head.

"How's your Couscous?" I asked.

"It's… I mean, it's not bad. It's good. But I was expecting better. The Tajine is fantastic, however."

"I agree, it's pretty good. Look, I need to ask you something," I said, sweating a little bit. Though, it was probably from the Tajine.

"You've been dying to tell me something ever since our bus ride. Is everything good?" she said.

"We've had our moments, right?" I said, trying to find the right words to say.

"What's that supposed to mean?"

"The crazy pool party at Grace's. Our first meet-up at that arcade by campus. That time I told you how I felt about you, by the track field. Moments, you know."

She looked at me, biting her lips and squinting her eyes. "Yeah. What is it, Blake?"

"I like to think of what's happening right now, right here in Casablanca, as one of those moments. I guess… Just… Why me, Corazón?"

She turned her head and looked down toward the floor. "I don't know," she said.

"I'll word it differently," I followed, trying to salvage the conversation.

But then, "NO!" she said, out of the blue. "That's not what I thought you were going to say."

"You don't want to speak about it, then?" I said.

"Let's just enjoy this. This moment," she said, in finality.

Soon after, James and Grace returned. They sat down and ordered dessert.

"Alright, you two, go up and dance. Grace and I got some talking to do," James said, looking at me, getting under my skin once more. He was good at that.

I got up and asked Corazón to dance. She accepted and we were at it. Though she and I had only danced together once before, it felt natural. Clearly, we had chemistry. As the Moroccan music got sexier—the only way I can describe it—she got closer to me. I held her, waist to waist, like Michael Buble's "Sway." And we swayed away. I certainly was a great dancer; an inherent quality as a result of my Caribbean origin, but Corazón seemed to possess a skill I didn't know she had.

"You are really good at this," I said.

"Why do you sound so surprised? I'm always spending time with you," she said, smiling.

"Who would've thought, you and me dancing in Casablanca?" Truly, such a thought I would've never fathomed. Yet, there we were, like Bogart and Bergman. "I'm going to say it once more, 'cause why the fuck not, Corazón. We are in fucking Casablanca and you are the girl who I want to spend the rest of my life with. Why can't this be the beginning of a beautiful friendship?" I let it all out. At that moment, I tried to kiss her, as if making it official, but she turned her head and followed to hug me.

"Don't say such silly things," Corazón said, with

watery eyes. "I'm going to go on a walk with Grace. There's a fortune teller around the corner I want to try. Maybe you and I can try it after, if I'm not tired."

"That's not fair. Now I have to kick it with... *James*."

"You'll be fine," she said. "I just need to clear my head."

"I get it. I'll see you back at the hotel then?"

"Yeah, sounds good," she said, as she and Grace headed out.

James, smirking for no apparent reason, walked up to me. He put his arm over my shoulder as if I was his "bro," truly an uncomfortable scene. "We need to talk, my simpy friend."

"What did you just call me?" I said, ready to throw the first punch.

"Admit it, Blake. Let's not lie to each other right now. What are you doing to yourself? It's almost as if you like the feeling of almost having what you want instead of, you know, having it? Better yet, you are like a hopeless romantic. You're an odd version of Romeo, hanging on to Juliet's rotting corpse like a fool. Or Gatsby, but poor, very poor."

I pushed him off me and he almost stumbled to the

ground. I was furious. But James was right. He wasn't an English major, but his metaphors were spot on. As crazy as it sounded, it seemed like James was coming from an honest perspective. He was trying to help me. It baffles me to this day.

"Walk with me, Blake. You and I have our differences. However, I've been in your shoes before."

James Calhoun, the ostentatious James Calhoun, was once in my shoes? That was a tough one to imagine, but somehow not so hard to believe. It scared me, though, that at the extreme end of the Blake spectrum was the James-type.

James continued preaching, "You are probably thinking of her as we are speaking right now, right?"

"Yeah, but not for the reasons you are suggesting. Look, I get you are trying to be of some help, but your evaluation of my circumstances is erroneous. I've told Corazón countless times how I feel."

"No. I'm right, Blake. You don't even call her by her real name. What the fuck does *Corazón* even mean? The fuck is that?"

I guess he had a point. He just couldn't understand the scope of my relationship with Corazón. I stuck around because she stuck around. How could one explain that? I was single and she was single. I loved her. Did she love me? Perhaps. Regardless, she was *mi Corazón*. In Spanish, quite literally, my heart. Figuratively, my love.

"Blake, you should've never come to Casablanca. That's the truth. I hate to say it, but this just makes your whole simpy thing with your *Cora*-whatever a whole lot worse. Here's some advice. Maybe she just wants something casual instead of a relationship. You know, to fuck. And you are making it difficult. Ask her. Go ahead. When we go back to the hotel, call her and ask her. Don't be a pussy."

That was the second time James had ever called me that. This time it didn't bother me. And as much as I had entertained the idea of her and I doing it for the first time, I was never going to ask Corazón for a random hook-up. College was behind me and that culture as well. What I wanted with Corazón was that Hollywood ending from all those '50s movies. I wanted romantic long talks, deep-rooted arguments that went full-circle, and visits from a partner, unannounced and unscripted. It's difficult to describe the state of our relationship at that point in time, but it was somewhat akin to the elegant back-and-forth between James Stewart and Grace Kelly in *Rear Window*. That's how I'd always imagined Corazón, like the Princess of Monaco.

When we got back to the hotel it was almost midnight. Grace and Corazón were not back yet, so James invited me for drinks. We sat in his room's balcony, looking out into the lively streets of busy Casablanca. Even this late at night, the city was alive.

"How's the scotch?" asked James.

"Tastes like scotch," I said, with a laugh. "Thanks."

"You know she's talking to Grace about you, right? That conversation we had, she's having it with Grace."

"Let me guess. You and Grace planned this," I asked, sarcastically.

"Damn it, Blake. Why are you so naïve? One doesn't spend hours at a fortune teller for the sake of it. You like movies, right? Fortune tellers in movies cater to your love life with magic cards while they steal your money. Like in *Ghost*."

I laughed. "I didn't know you were a Patrick Swayze fan."

"I'm serious." James took a long sip from his scotch

and cleared his throat. He really was serious. "When she comes back, it's game-on. Either you'll receive what you've always wanted or live the rest of your life not knowing what could've been."

"James, now *you* sound like a fortune teller," I said, thinking perhaps the scotch was the one truly speaking.

"You need to tell her what you want. And make her understand," he said.

"What makes you think this time will be any different from the countless times I've opened my heart to Corazón?"

James looked at me with a certainty I'd never seen before in a man I hardly knew. "Because she's going to tell you the same thing."

I too was under the influence of that rather tasty Moroccan scotch, and as dazed as I was, James' words hit me as clear as day. I felt that. Motivation just seemed to sprout of nowhere, as if filling a bottomless pit. Nevertheless, there was nothing I could tell Corazón that she didn't already know. The challenge was to make her understand, and ultimately, to help her make a choice.

"Look over there. You see that guy, with the red

bandana covering his face," said James. He was pointing over the balcony to a street vendor. Selling flowers at night seemed odd, but then again, lovestruck tourists are the ones roaming Casablanca at midnight. "I wonder what kind of person would buy flowers this late at night? And for what occasion…"

I took one last sip from my scotch. "Alright, alright. *That* person would be me? I get it." I laughed. "But you know, if I do that, it totally contradicts everything you've said."

James smiled, like Mr. Miyagi. "You've learned." He continued. "I'll text Grace and tell her I'll be in the lobby. You and your Corazón can settle the score right here. You've got home field advantage at this point."

I cracked a smile. "It's also a terrific scene. What a view."

He placed his arm over my shoulder, again, like a bro. "That too, that too."

James left right after. I couldn't believe the bond we had just created. Just like that, over scotch in Casablanca. Corazón texted me then, confirming she was coming up shortly. My eyes were transfixed by the view in front of me, but I was certain the scotch was mostly to blame. I took one last look at busy Casablanca before closing my eyes and taking a breather. To sing or not to sing. That was the test ahead of me. One last song, one last poem, one last pitch for Corazón. *Que sera, sera*. I was ready.

Corazón walked into the room. She walked toward the balcony and sat where James once did. I didn't know why, but I felt the urge to place my left hand over her right hand. She then took it a step further, sliding her hand under mine, interlocking fingers. We smiled at each other and soon smiles turned into quick laughter. Our hands retreated. I followed it with a heart hand-gesture, right over my chest. She smiled again, but this time, as the grin on her face relaxed, I couldn't help but notice that it wasn't a smile of joy, but one of something else.

"I know how you feel. It's lovely to have people who love you. Who think of you in high regards. Who put you on a pedestal, no matter the imperfections," Corazón said, with a tear running down her cheek. "And I love that. I adore that. That you have me on this pedestal, like a goddess. Blake, I love the feeling of being loved. I… can't thank you enough for making me feel like a million bucks. That's why I want you here, with me."

I too had a tear running down my face, which soon multiplied to many. "I'm happy to hear that," I said. "Then why, Corazón. No… Elizabeth. Why, Elizabeth, can't we be together? I need you to understand that this is real."

"Blake, that's the thing. It isn't. Listen to me carefully. Everything I've said; it's true. Still, that doesn't deny the fact that you are not in love with *me*. You are in love with *your* version of me."

Was she right? It took me by surprise, but Elizabeth had somehow deciphered me. I didn't know what to feel, yet it made sense.

"That doesn't change a thing," I said. Even though I stood by that statement, deep inside me I knew it was the wrong thing to say.

"I will never be good for you, Blake. For that, I rather live by the edge of that road that leads to the two of us. Savoring the journey, prolonging it, 'til the end of time. I'd hate to reach that destination, disappoint you, disappoint me, and lose us forever. Do you understand?" She was crying now, and so was I.

I looked down toward the floor, trying to hide away the pain. I understood then that this was our last moment. I didn't want it to be, but she had already made her choice. Now it was time to make mine.

I chose my words carefully. "I will never stop thinking the way I think about you. But sooner rather than later, a journey must reach that destination. I wanted to arrive with you by my side. And perhaps I'll never stop loving you, but I can't live on the sidelines forever, without you, truly." I stopped. Then, as much as it hurt, as much as I didn't want to admit it, I said my last goodbyes. "Sadly, it's not true that all we've got is time."

Elizabeth stood up as she wiped the tears from her eyes. She understood. I stood up next, completely transformed. We gave each other one last look, a warm embrace, before calling it a night.

As she left toward the door, "The fortune teller said I'd be going on an adventure tomorrow. Funny enough, minutes later Grace won another giveaway. Tickets to a resort in Marrakech. She's a lucky girl. If I don't see you tomorrow, that's why." Then, as she opened the door, she stopped and looked back. "*Adiós*, Blake."

The Bohemians

I smiled, waved back, and saw her leave into that good night.

Ch. 5

John

Merci

MERCI

The Bohemians

—

Time is memory, or rather, time is to remember. It's been a long time since my first European adventure, but as I look back to the moments that defined me, I can't help myself to fully reminisce. Of what exactly? Or who? Quite frankly, of *her*. My first love. And where? Of all places, in Paris.

I was one of the lucky fellows in our department who was picked for the school's foreign exchange program. I'd never left the country. The only state besides my own I'd ever visited was New York. So, this was a big deal. I was terrified. And not because I'd be stepping inside a plane for the very first time, but because Lauren was going to sit next to me. I didn't like Lauren. She was despicable, with no sense of humor whatsoever, so I'd heard. The thought of a 10-hour flight with Despicable Lauren seemed like torture. But this was non-negotiable. I couldn't trade seats because no one wanted my seat. Lauren was not a very kind person, or so it seemed. There were stories that she let a student drown by the campus lake during freshman year because she didn't want to get her new dress wet. It was all the gossip on campus for weeks. The deceased's family even tried to sue her. Who knows what really happened and if she was at fault for that kid's death, but ever since that day the entire university learned the name *Lauren Lancaster*. I certainly didn't want to talk to her. But she had other ideas.

I had the window seat. With big headphones on, I closed my eyes and blasted my music. The message was clear: "Leave me alone, Lauren." Then she pinched my arm. I acted as if I didn't feel it, but then the pinch turned to a reserved punch.

"Lauren, I'm trying to sleep. It's a long flight," I said.

"You're going to sleep the entire flight?" she asked.

I paused for a second. "Yes."

"You don't like me, do you?" she said, reading my body language.

"Not many people do, Lauren," I said, unmoved.

She sat back deep into her seat and closed her eyes. A tear peeking out.

"Why are you crying now?"

"I didn't know what to do," she said, sobbing.

I couldn't believe it. Lauren had decided to grow a heart at that exact moment, right before takeoff.

"Lauren, I don't have time to listen to your excuses. He's dead. You could've stopped that. Or at least jumped into the lake; do something. But you didn't. Why? Who the fuck knows." I couldn't believe I had just said that. Even I felt some type of guilt for speaking so frankly.

"Because if I had jumped, I would've died too."

I didn't understand what she meant. But then it hit me.

"You can't swim."

"Yeah," she said.

From there on she told me her side of the story: things that never came to light when the whole university cracked down on her like a witch-hunt. I too had jumped quick to misjudge her. Clearly, she just needed someone to listen to her. There was nothing she could've done. I still wanted to fall asleep and wake up to the shaking of the plane as it landed in France, but Lauren just kept talking and talking. While I no longer saw her as "Despicable Lauren," becoming her friend never crossed my mind and I wanted to keep it that way. I believed her story; mostly because I too didn't know how to swim. Perhaps I would've reacted the same way in a similar situation: in pure shock. However, our similarities ended there. We had nothing else in common. Yet, she went on.

"Do you like movies? Films?" she said.

Obviously, I wasn't going to sleep a full 10 hours. What a feat that would be. I decided to entertain the question and see where the conversation would lead. "I do. Both movies and films. There's a difference."

She replied, excited. "Yes! Someone gets it! I've been debating this for the longest time. So, what's your favorite? Movie and film."

"It fits that our destination's France. Favorite movie is *Midnight in Paris*. Film is *Cleo from 5 to 7* by Agnes Varda," I said.

"You're kidding, right? I'm a huge Agnes Varda fan," she said.

Apparently, we had some things in common. I never really got into the whole French Cinema hype but watching Varda's film changed how I perceived the world. Not many films can do that and when they do, they tend to become your favorite. Even though *Cleo from 5 to 7* was my favorite film—a film about a woman learning she has terminal cancer—that was the only

Agnes Varda movie I'd seen. If Lauren was going to ramble on about all the Varda films that had transformed her cultural perspective then there was nothing for me to contribute to the conversation, other than just to listen and take it all in. However, she threw a sudden curveball in our now rather interesting small talk.

"I'll be honest, I completely hate *Cleo from 5 to 7*. Not to be harsh, just honest, it's boring."

"I thought you said you were a Varda fan," I said, flabbergasted. "How could you not like *Cleo*? It's quite literally her best film. Probably the best film coming out of the French New Wave. Come on, you must be fucking around with me."

She wasn't. "I'm serious. I don't find it enjoyable and it has no substance besides its feminist ideology."

"Really?" I said, looking at her, trying to understand how she of all people wouldn't connect with the film.

"What's there to take in? She goes on a selfish trip around Paris before finding out her fate. Meets some guy and supposedly falls in love. Wishful thinking and unrealistic. That's what I think," Lauren said.

I shook my head. "I've never heard that take on *Cleo*.

I think it's pretty realistic to want to fall in love or do something stupid before finding out if today is going to be your last day on Earth."

She didn't like my answer and just stared at me for about a minute. I didn't mean to suggest that Cleo's ordeal in the movie was at all related to Lauren's whole debacle at the lake, but there she was thinking just that. I had it coming, I guess. And to some extent, maybe that was what I was suggesting, subconsciously. It didn't matter anymore; Lauren moved on to the next subject.

"*Midnight in Paris* is a funny movie," she said.

"Finally, something we can agree with," I said.

She continued. "But I can't help but think that the movie is all about Woody and his own frustrations about the modern Hollywood system."

"Aren't all his movies about himself? I'd argue every piece of writing, every conflict and every subject matter is a representation or a reflection of the author's frustration of something in his or her life." Even I was impressed with my own response.

"That was very elegantly put," Lauren said. We went back and forth on many other movies and films throughout the flight, arguing left and right and reaching consensus on plenty of occasions. So much time had passed that we were already approaching Paris, ready to land.

"So, where are you staying while we take classes in French for two weeks?" she said.

"Close by. Near the school. Nice old couple is taking me in. They are Spaniards so I'll be speaking Spanish, mostly."

"Hit me up sometime. We don't have much time left and Paris is beautiful," she said.

I smiled. "I'll think about it." We went our separate ways as we exited the airport. The Spanish couple was already waiting for me in the lobby, so after greeting them we quickly left for the busy streets of Paris.

The French itinerary was simple. I was to attend class from eight a.m. to three p.m. Right after at around four-thirty p.m. I was to play soccer with some local students. Then at six p.m. I'd make my way back to the Spaniards to shower and clean myself up for a drive-in movie at eight p.m. in a locale near the Eiffel Tower. That's how it pretty much went for the first week and a half. I had forgotten all about Lauren. But then, just a few days before the trip's end while at dinner with the

Spaniards, Agnes Varda once again became the subject of conversation. The Spaniards confessed that they absolutely loved the auteur back when they roamed Madrid amid Franco's regime. Sometimes they had to bribe some Spanish cops to smuggle her films across the border due to the government's tight censorship on foreign entertainment. It was fascinating what they had to do just to see their favorite motion pictures. Appropriately, Lauren came to mind. I texted her as soon as I finished dinner and after apologizing for reaching out so late into our trip, we made plans for the following night.

It was eight p.m. when I met Lauren by a local café not too far from the Eiffel Tower. She looked splendid. Lauren was a pretty woman, a little above average but nothing like the Victoria's Secret models that stole my attention any time I passed by the sorority clubs on campus. That night, though, I saw her in a different light. The setting definitely had an effect, as the Parisian nightlife contrasted well Lauren's dark brunette hair. She wore tight blue jeans with a white top and a black leather jacket. Looking back, she almost looked like Sandy from *Grease*. She had already bought coffee for the two of us and insisted on walking the streets instead of sitting down like normal people do. I wasn't complaining. For once, this was a conversation I was looking forward to, even though I had no idea what the subject would be. I took a leap of faith and set the night in motion.

"First of all, thanks for meeting with me tonight. I'm terribly sorry that I took this long to hit you up."

"We're busy people. I should've reached out myself as well. So, it's both our faults," she said.

"I guess, but not necessarily. The good thing is we are here now, right? It all worked out," I said. I started to sip a little faster from my coffee. As we walked on, she kept bumping into me, slightly but rather playfully.

"I'm going to ask you something, Johnny. And forgive me if I'm being direct," she said.

"Sure, go on," I said, intrigued.

"Back in the plane, were you comparing Cleo to me? Was I supposed to understand her situation because of... You know?

"I wasn't. But come to think of it, perhaps I unknowingly suggested it. In any case, it prompted you to think of it that way, so I'm sorry."

"It's fine. I saw the film again this past week. My thoughts have changed about it," she said, with a slight smile. She looked at me and continued. "You and I are similar in that we somewhat think alike, in rather philosophical ways. It dawned on me as I watched *Cleo* that she and I have similar tragedies."

"What do you mean," I said, confused.

"She fell in love," Lauren said, looking down toward the ground.

I felt a deep cold rise from the bottom of my stomach up to the center of my chest as she uttered those words. Almost as if by fate, we also had just entered the vicinity of the Trocadero Garden. Its fountain sprinkling endless water, forming beautiful aqua formations. A confession of love couldn't happen at a much perfect place. I, though, was not feeling the same way. And that gutted me. I obviously felt something. I was attracted to her, both physically and philosophically, as she put it. But I didn't love her. I'd never loved anyone. At least not like that, romantically. When it came to romance I had never held a good batting average. I'd always find ways to strike out at every at-bat. I've hit a few doubles, but never a home run. However, those instances involved me being at the mercy of the pitcher's fastball. Now I was on the mound and I didn't want to break her heart, like all the other girls who'd broken mine. Lauren didn't deserve it. And so...

"Have you ever fallen in love, Johnny?" Lauren asked out of the blue.

"I... can't say that I have," I said, careful in my tone of voice.

"Really? That can't be right?"

"I've had my heart broken several times, but I don't think that counts as me having been in love," I said.

"But don't you have to be in love for your heart to get broken?" Lauren said, in a smart counter.

"You've got a point. Lauren, look, I don't want to break your heart." I had to be direct, just as she was with me. I wouldn't allow myself to lead her on, only to destroy her like me and all the other students had already done back in freshman year. Not again. Then, again, she surprised me.

"I'm not in love with you, Johnny. Perhaps you misunderstood me."

"Oh... Well, you've lost me, Lauren," I said, laughing

right afterward.

She joined me in laughter and soon after held my hand. "Cleo fell in love, but only for a day if we assume she meets her fate when credits roll. We could do the same, right now. Tomorrow we leave for Connecticut, Johnny. Forget Vegas, what happens in Paris, stays in Paris."

I understood. At that moment time became like a ripple in a pond, only literally. Lauren and I jumped into the Trocadero, seemingly forgetting that we both couldn't swim.

"I know it sounds harsh and maybe a tad inappropriate, but don't let me die in Paris," I said, as I kissed her under the massive backdrop of the night's translucent Eiffel Tower.

It was midnight when Lauren and I decided to fall in love for just a moment. Midnight in Paris, how ironic. I found it odd that just a few seconds later fireworks lit up the dark sky, almost as if the universe was celebrating this brief moment in time.

"We should get out of the water, avoid the deep," Lauren said.

I agreed and after drying ourselves we laid down on

the Trocadero, looking up as the fireworks continued beyond the Eiffel Tower. Lauren and I spoke of many things that night, yet I don't remember what any of us said. Even to this day as I try and lose myself in time, in memory, I fail to grasp what she told me at the Trocadero. Our kiss lasted seconds, but that feeling of love was forever kept in the void of time, the tree of memory.

When I returned to the Spaniards that night, now past midnight, I had trouble falling asleep. My feelings for Lauren hadn't changed, yet when she opened up to me I felt the need to abide by her desires. Perhaps I've always wanted to be loved and indirectly saw myself in Lauren's shoes? That somehow, if our roles were reversed I would've wanted her to do the same for me. I didn't regret what had happened, but I also didn't comprehend the severity of it all, or rather, the implications. Was I supposed to stay in contact with Lauren? Would she want me to contact her at all, despite her suggestion that whatever we felt would cease to exist post our flight back to school? Conundrum after conundrum. My mind just wandered, but sooner rather than later I had to close my eyes and wake up early that same day to fly back to America.

After I said my goodbyes that morning to the Spaniards, a taxi picked me up and took me to the airport. I gave Paris one last look and headed toward my gate. This time I didn't sit next to Lauren. I didn't see her at all in the plane. Yet, the entire flight back to Connecticut I couldn't get her off my mind. Again, I sat by the window seat and as I looked down at Paris from above, I focused my sight on that dear old spot in the Trocadero Garden where Lauren and I fell in love. What a sight it was from the sky. Two young lovers—sad lovers—with nothing in common but a fancy French movie and a fear of the deep.

The semester continued without Lauren in sight. Even though I still had her number, and she had mine, we never texted, never called each other. It was probably fear that kept me from reaching out. The fear of what? That I do not know. I always figured she kept her distance in honor of her word, and to that I was right. Almost out of pure coincidence I saw Lauren again by that campus lake that brought her so much pain, and from which I first became aware of her existence.

"It's been a long, long time," she said, with a smile

on her face.

"It has, indeed." I followed to hug her and as we embraced, her hold was strong, almost as if she didn't want to let go.

"You have no idea what you did for me that day in Paris, Johnny," Lauren said, with a playful voice. "Just to be clear, and I hope you feel the same way, I didn't expect you to hit me up or anything, or fall in love or whatever. But please, never forget that in that speck of a moment I truly fell in love."

I already knew all of that, but what took me by surprise was what came right after.

"I felt like Cleo when I got on that plane, and like a Hollywood movie, I wanted my movie to go out with a spectacle, and there's no better setting than that of France. I'm glad my... film didn't end." She then turned to me and with a heavy accent, the likes of Cleo herself, Lauren said, "Merci."

It all hit me instantaneously. A tear swam down my cheek as I placed my hand on her shoulder. "And there's plenty more films to see."

Ch. 6

Machu Picchu

MACHU PICCHU

The Bohemians

—

Carlos; he was bigger then. I often think of our times on campus, fooling around in my dorm. Of all things, he always spoke about his ridiculous crush on Sally and how much she meant to him. I told him how preposterous it was to keep such feelings inside. He should've told Sally his truth. But he didn't. He waited for so long until it was too late. I wish he had looked at me in the same way he always looked at her Instagram posts. I don't know how to explain it, but it was beautiful. The way he'd describe her would always make me tear up. (I'm sentimental like that.) He'd always find it weird, though. I guess, most likely, because I never met Sally during our college days.

After graduation, after his affection for Sally had somewhat dissipated, I hung out with Carlos from time to time, trying to get him to open up to "new" things. Drugs was a subject he never wanted to touch. However, I knew that if I could convince him to join me on my trip to Peru, then perhaps being closer to the ayahuasca tree would pressure him into challenging his convictions.

In the ancient scriptures of the Inca, my ancestors described in detail how a person's mind can enter another's using the magical ayahuasca herb. The ritual required that the wandering individual—the one navigating the other's mind—first perform an action toward the other which would render them submissive. This was essential. Not only because having two "Wanderers" could break both persons' minds to the point of madness, but also, and most importantly, because I was an unwedded woman. According to the scriptures, the celestial connection of husband and wife made the partners "one with the herb; submissive by design." A husband submits to his wife by accepting to go forth with the ritual, and vice versa. Carlos was not my husband and I clearly wasn't his wife. Making him accept to go forth with the ritual was obviously not going to work. Luckily, even in the days of the Inca there were curious women like me. The scriptures gave me a blueprint to my goal, and to my benefit, it involved something Carlos and I had done many times before in my college dorm.

"I am NOT going to the outskirts of Peru. I'm a city-guy, not a Peruvian jungle-guy," said Carlos, as I showed him the two plane tickets I had already bought. "Why are you doing this to me? That's not fair."

I knew the only way to get him to come with me to Peru was to hit him with the guilt card. Carlos was a cash freak; he hated to see money badly spent. With tickets in hand, there was zero chance he would make them go to waste.

"Okay, you win, goddammit. I'll go to Peru with you. I want to visit Machu Picchu."

"We'll see. I really want us to go to this jungle. A hike of sorts," I said.

"What's so important about this specific jungle?" said Carlos, eyebrows up.

"According to textbooks, it's an ancient Inca burial ground. Lots of statues and relics. You know how much I love history."

"Yeah, me too. I still want to visit Machu Picchu."

The following week we boarded our plane and landed in Lima around midnight. We slept in separate rooms at a nearby motel before catching a bus to the remote jungle. I was hoping that Carlos and I would sleep together beforehand, as practice for the ritual, but he insisted on having his own room. I guess he was just tired. It would've saved us money to room together, but apparently, the Peruvian peso was so low against the dollar that sleeping solo didn't dent our budget one bit.

Even though our college days were long gone, it seemed like Carlos still had those same feelings for Sally. I assumed so because he still carried that same Hawaiian keychain she gave him some time after graduation. He left it in his car, in the airport parking lot, but why keep such a gift for so long if not for it having sentimental value? I asked him about it on our way to the Inca jungle.

"What's up with you and that Sally girl?" I said, keeping it casual.

"What?"

"The girl of your dreams. That's what you called her, right?"

He shook his head and smiled. "I hope she's okay. We haven't caught up in quite some time."

"How long has it been?" I asked.

"Three years since we last spoke," said Carlos.

"She was your world way back when, and now?" I said, digging for more information.

"I was a very different person all those years ago, but

even that Carlos was malleable. She helped me become the person I am today. For that, I'm grateful."

I wanted to dig for more, but I knew unearthing his past feelings for Sally would make my goal a pain to attain. We arrived at the jungle some minutes after. There was a route we were supposed to take, one the bus driver said was "important not to deviate from." Getting lost in the Peruvian jungle meant death: snakes, dengue mosquitoes, poisonous frogs, those types of life-threatening things. I appreciated the bus driver's concern, but I had my own plans.

We hiked for about thirty minutes. We stopped by a nearby tree because Carlos had to pee. (Oh, men.)

"What are you *doing?*" Carlos said, while doing his business.

I stood right beside him. "You know, just taking a peek." I then laughed, trying to target his insecurities.

"I know what you are trying to do," he said. "Can I just pee in peace?"

"Oh my God, are you getting aroused?!?" I laughed even harder now.

He quickly zipped his pants. "Geez." He then laughed as well.

"You know… I was thinking… You've heard of the 'Mile High Club,' right?" I said, now that his mind was in the right place.

He countered. "Let's keep walking. Before it gets too dark."

Carlos didn't want to talk about it, but I had already planted the seed in his mind. Little by little, as we walked, we deviated from the route and started nearing the Inca site.

"Come on! Not many people have joined the 'Mile High Club.' I think the same can be said for 'The Jungle Club.' I made up the phrase but you know what I mean, Carlos."

He looked at me, amazed. "You want to fuck in the jungle?"

"Yes. Why not?" I said. The question was funny, but he seemed surprised that I was insinuating it. We hadn't done it for some time, perhaps six months, but most of our time together in college started like that: hookups. Except I was the fool who started catching feelings. He would open up to me and I to him. We started getting close. That's how I learned of Sally. After graduation, we still kept close, hooking up on the weekends. He then got a job in New York and I rarely saw him.

"You know it's going to be uncomfortable, right? All them twigs," he said.

"It doesn't have to be. I've clearly thought this through so just let me handle this, okay."

We arrived at the Inca location some twenty minutes after. My ayahuasca concoction was in my hiking bag. I purchased it from a local dealer during the night, by the motel, when Carlos was asleep. The dealer also gave me a picture of a plant, and instructions on how to combine it with his product. The fresher the herb, the stronger the reaction, so I needed to make the ritualistic drink on the spot. There was only one way this was going to work. If Carlos had seen me mixing drugs prior to us having sex, then he would've most definitely freaked and the trip would've all been for nothing. Unbeknownst to Carlos, I found the plant, discreetly, and after a quick prayer—to avoid any bad omens—all was relinquished.

We started slow, taking our clothes off section by section. The moon was setting and night falling.

"Should we make our tents first?" Carlos said.

"Shut up. You're ruining the moment."

We then kissed, our clothes off, naked. By now I was on top, in full control. It truly was a romantic scene, as I had hoped. The ritual didn't call for a full moon and the night sky, but I must admit that it made it even better, almost as if it was meant to happen exactly like this. His eyes were closed as pleasure ensued. With the herb now under my tongue and the concoction in my hand, I took a sip, and with the liquid still in my mouth as I mixed both within, I leaned down toward Carlos and kissed him, letting the ayahuasca flow from one mouth to the other. I kept kissing him, forcing him to take it all down, without room for a breath. Even more intense were the movement of my hips, as now the ayahuasca was taking control of my body. After one more intense ride, I let him breathe, his eyes indescribable, but a smile on his face. I was also happy. Immensely happy, like I'd never been. Then, we both relaxed. Or, rather, our minds. We weren't in Peru anymore. No, *I* wasn't in Peru anymore. All I could see was my old dorm room, and a bar, and a movie theater, and Sally.

  The residence hall looked the same, except for the many rotating geometric shapes that replaced the walls encasing me. Students roamed freely. Yet, Carlos was nowhere to be seen. I soon approached my dorm door and when I opened it, I saw myself on the other side. Yet, my other-self didn't recognize that she was *me*. Rather...

"Carlos, why are you looking at me like that?" My other-self said.

I started to cry, of joy. The ritual had worked! My other-self, though, just stood concerned. I snapped right out of it. I couldn't help but notice how beautiful she looked. *Was this how Carlos always imagined me?* I was more attractive during my college years, but not like this woman in front of me.

"You look so pretty," I said, losing myself in my eyes.

"Carlos... Ah..." My other-self looked at me so strangely.

I realized then that Carlos had never complimented me like I had just done. We would talk about everything and everyone but never about us. I realized I was making my dreams come true with what I had just said. But this wasn't why I was here. I didn't want to break her magic, *our* magic, but unfortunately...

"Have you seen Sally? Is she in the building? Outside?" I said.

That devastated other-me. I knew it because just saying those words hurt me-me. In real life, there was no way of me knowing of Sally's whereabouts. But this was Carlos' mind and that woman in front of me was not really me. His subconscious would give me everything.

Reluctantly, other-me gave me a lead. She pointed toward the wall next to me.

"You want me to walk over there?" I asked.

Other-me nodded and I proceeded. I placed my hand on the geometric shapes in front of me before attempting any weird "magic." My hand, and then my arm, went right through the wall, like slime, or gelatin. The wall then changed its form, as if a portal had opened, expanding outward from the circumference of my arm, the hole on the wall I had just made. On the other side was a bar. But this bar was no ordinary bar. When I walked into it, inverted beer tornadoes sat on the bar stools. They seemed to have a mind of their own: sentient alcohol. They conversed with each other. Others shouted as they watched a soccer match on top of the tongue of some random soccer player I didn't recognize; Argentinian perhaps. His head was the TV in this dreamscape; his tongue the screen. A number of attractive blonde women sat by a nearby table. One of them flirted with a beer tornado while the tallest of them all, approximately seven feet from top to bottom, with massive toned legs, just stared at me with a blank look. She called for me and as I approached her, pointed toward a jukebox. Another blonde woman stood in front of it. She was different from the rest. For one, she felt real. She didn't speak with sentient alcohol weather machinations or had gigantic physical features. She was just normal, looking for a song to play. This was *her*, finally.

"Sally?" I said.

She turned around. Suddenly time seemed to slow down. Light radiated from somewhere and her hair just flowed, perfectly. It was cinematic. She was gorgeous, just like her Instagram photos. Carlos hadn't changed, or upgraded, a single feature.

"Heyyy, stranger?" she said, with a contagious smile. "Help me pick a song."

Manic pixie dream girl. Those words were running through my head as Sally stood there like a Hollywood lead. But she wasn't one. I was sure about it. Perhaps out there, in the real world, through Carlos' outspoken words, she was like Zoey from *500 Days of Summer*. But not in here where it mattered: his mind.

"Sure, Sally. Let's see," I said.

The jukebox had all the songs I hated. Unsurprisingly, these were the songs Carlos adored. Frank Sinatra, Dean Martin, Andy Williams; all these old rats were there. As I scanned each song title, some invisible force seemed to guide my hand toward the Dean Martin's. I, or it, picked the song "From The Bottom of My Heart."

As the song played, "Ain't that a little too obvious?" said Sally. "Come on, you don't have to hide it. You can say it now."

I wasn't sure what to say. Yet, I also knew what *had* to be said. I wasn't sure anymore if I was in some type of abstract dream created by Carlos' mind, or if this was actually a memory. *Was I reliving one of Carlos' memories about Sally?* I let that invisible force help me once again.

"You stole my heart since the first day I saw you," I said, all so eerily natural, as if I meant it. I was sure Carlos had, many years ago, but not me-me. It felt so strange.

"Why do you love me?" Sally said.

"Because you taught me to love myself," I said, now with tears in my eyes. *Carlos said that?* I couldn't believe it.

A sudden flash then wiped through my eyes and I couldn't see a thing. When I opened them, I saw Sally playing football with another man (a much older man) I didn't recognize. We were in a park now. Sally ran with the football tucked within her arms. The man then tackled her down and started tickling her, as they both laughed. This was then followed by a kissing session. *Carlos, what is this?* Then the football hit me on the head.

"You are supposed to catch that, buddy," the older man said.

"Right." I picked up the ball and threw it back to him.

"Over here," said Sally.

The man threw it to her and again went running after her. *Oh no…* This was another memory.

"Why did you do this to yourself?!?" I thought. *"What are you trying to achieve? This is torture."*

The older guy then approached me. "Hey man, thanks for coming along. Sally and I are going off to

Lyon after tomorrow, so I really appreciate you being here for her. She's really going to miss you."

I smiled. That's all I was able to do.

I was disappointed. I understood now why he cared so much for Sally, but everything has its limits. He appreciated her to the point of self-deprecation. Even I would've looked the other way if he had those feelings for me.

I felt the invisible force again, but I was now able to somehow control it. It was pulling me toward a nearby car—perhaps, in this memory, Carlos left after the brief talk with the man. Maybe this was the last time he saw her—but I had some words to say to Sally.

"Why are you marrying this man?" I said. I had no idea if that was the case, but it turned out to be true.

"We've talked about this. I love him," she said.

"Did you ever love me? Like you love him?" I said.

"You can't ask me that. Not now," she said, emotionless.

"In the past. What about in the past?"

Sally looked confused. "In the past?"

"In college, Sally. Did you love me in college?" I said, feeling a rumble under my feet.

Sally wouldn't say. The shake under my feet grew stronger.

"Time to go…" she said.

The earthquake split the ground in two, forming a downward slope that dragged me down to the abyss. I wasn't afraid. I now floated in endless darkness. I could hear the sound of music, though. It was growing louder, and after a bit, it was no longer indistinguishable. It was Dean Martin's "Blue Moon." Gravity returned just as quickly, pulling me down to a light of sorts. When I stopped "falling," I found myself sitting comfortably on a recliner seat. The light was coming from an enormous projector screen in front of me. I was in a movie theater. I wasn't alone, however. What I saw next truly amazed me. To my left was Dean Martin.

"Young man, how was that?" Dean said, jolly as I'd seen him in Carlos' Criterion Collection.

"Ahh… 'Blue Moon?' You mean you were singing that live? Like right now? That wasn't a jukebox? A recording?"

He smiled. "I appreciate the compliment, young man."

This wasn't a memory. Of course it wasn't.

"The movie won't start for a few minutes and it seems we've got the theater to ourselves. I point out the obvious because I'd like to ask you a question, young man?" Dean said, sincerely.

"Ask ahead, Mr. Martin," I said, unsure as to how to honor him.

"Deano! Call me Deano," he laughed. "I can see that something is bothering you. I can tell from experience that it's about a girl. I am right, aren't I?"

"Well, yes. I'm disappointed. I'm angry that my friend loves this girl, even though she's moved on entirely. Why can't *he*? Why does he keep after her when she clearly doesn't love him back and has never felt the way he feels? It just doesn't make sense."

Deano looked at me. "Are we really talking about a *friend?*"

I locked eyes with him. "Yes, Deano." Of course I was talking about Carlos, but how could he have known?

"Well, young man, all I can say is this: Love is strange. Some men go on with their lives living faithfully with one woman, while their heart rests with another. Love was never meant to be reciprocal, but it's a hell of a good time when it is."

Smiling, I said, "Ain't that a kick in the head?"

"A great song, indeed." Deano then stood up. "Feels wrong to see a movie without some popcorn. Want some?"

I nodded. "That'd be great, Deano."

He left and now I was alone. What a trip. I knew he wasn't coming back. It was the end of the reel.

When I woke up next to Carlos, he was already up. We were both staring at the moon.

"Did you drug me?" He said.

"Yes," I said.

"Shit, Freddy was right. Damn... That was the best sex of my life."

I laughed. "You don't remember anything?"

"Not really. Just a feeling." He turned to me. "What time is it?"

I got up and reached for my hiking bag, then took out my phone. "Twenty-two minutes…"

"What?" Carlos said, surprised.

"We were knocked out for like twenty-two minutes."

"That… didn't feel like twenty-two minutes. More like an eternity."

"Yup. That's ayahuasca," I said.

"You gave me *what???*"

I knew he was going to freak out as soon as I told him.

"I could've *died!* Or worse, gone brain dead!"

"Higher chance by a snake or dengue mosquito really," I said, as if no big deal.

He was right, however.

We then clothed up, made our tents, and fell asleep again. The next morning, we retraced our steps and took a bus back to Lima. It was a quiet bus ride as we were both pretty tired.

"Machu Picchu can wait," he said.

The flight back to New York was the same. When we reached the parking lot and got in his car, the first thing Carlos reached for was that Hawaiian keychain.

"Why didn't you take it with you? To Peru?" I asked.

"I could've lost it."

I then reached over and kissed him.

"What was that for?" he said.

"Love was never meant to be reciprocal… I'll take my chances."

Ch. 7

Katelyn

2020

2020

—

In her time of need Katelyn looked no further than to Sophie's charm: her tarot deck. She was her confidant when it really mattered. Sophie listened, in silence, and Katelyn just vented, wholeheartedly. On one particular girls' night, however, in a hibachi restaurant in Downtown Los Angeles, Katelyn seemed distraught. The last time Sophie saw such emotions from her best friend was many years ago, before Lloyd, when Katelyn left behind her first love, a guy named Alejandro, in Barcelona. She adored the old Spanish city during her study-abroad college semester, however, she was young and couldn't see herself building a life in a culture so different from her own. *What could it be now?* The two besties ordered cocktails before Katelyn began to unwind.

"It's just you, me, and the chef tonight," said Katelyn, examining her surroundings.

The chef smiled under his transparent face shield. "Pandemic is keeping our customers away. Let me rephrase that. The governor is…" He stopped himself. "Thank you for joining us tonight, ladies. Whenever you are ready, the grill is at your service."

They all smiled, acknowledging the eerie state of the world.

Katelyn turned to Sophie. With a sip of her cocktail, "I had an awful dream last night."

Sophie took a sip as well. "What happened?"

"I was in my office in Venus Trap, *trapped*. How funny, right? And then I died, unfulfilled. As if years passed and I didn't achieve anything. I was just there until I became a rotting corpse." She paused. "I woke up with this feeling. Like, there's something missing, or a realization of something. It just made me angry. Because I'm doing everything I can to get out, but nothing happens. Now my dreams are giving me cautionary tales."

"You've been trying to leave that job for as long as I can remember. Any luck with offers, Kate?"

"No. Not even callbacks. It's as if I'm worthless to these automated resume-scanning bots…" She then sighed. "I sound ungrateful. I know. I'm lucky to be employed right now; I get it. And maybe that's just it. Maybe that feeling is survivor's guilt. In a way. Does that make sense?"

Sophie nodded.

"Perhaps… Look, I'm not ashamed to have a job right now, while others don't. Just that I'm not happy with the job that I have. Especially when everything was going just right before the universe decided to fuck us for a year."

"I see," said Sophie.

"Venus is a good company. Our streaming initiatives paid off, big time. But guess who came knocking at my door in February? I'll tell you… Warner Bros."

Sophie finished her cocktail. "Fuck, Kate. I'm sorry."

"See! I get the call of a lifetime and the next day God says, 'Fuck you, Kate. Pandemic coming at ya…'" Katelyn then finished her drink.

Sophie smiled. "Kate, maybe the dream *is* a cautionary tale. But of something different. What about that boy who works with you… Is it maybe *that*, that's bothering you? Maybe your dream, your subconscious, is giving you a hint…"

"I don't know," Katelyn said. "Maybe."

"What's his name again?"

"Freddy," said Katelyn. "Back in February I never really thought of what would happen to him if I left

Venus. Even after what happened in that hotel months before. I guess current world events give you a new perspective."

"Do you like him?" asked Sophie.

"I ask myself that question every morning."

"Then maybe you do. I have this motto of mine: 'If you have to think twice about it, then run with it.'"

Katelyn had a hard time agreeing to that, but she smiled nonetheless, appreciating Sophie's insights.

"Ready to order?" The chef said, with two knives in his hands.

After Katelyn and Sophie decided on their meals, the chef performed various dangerous-looking tricks while cooking a combination of shrimp and rice. Such tricks weren't enough to distract Katelyn from the thought of her employee.

"Death in a dream… This feeling is not about him. Not entirely," said Katelyn.

"Lloyd?" asked Sophie.

"No," said Katelyn. "But I am thinking of ending things."

"Like Alejandro?"

Katelyn nodded. "Maybe I need to focus on myself

more. Travel the world a bit more. Flights are cheaper now."

They laughed.

After a beat, "I'm leaving Venus, Sophie."

"I mean, we already know that. For a long time. This isn't new. Come on, Kate, what's really on your mind? Why are you angry?"

Katelyn pondered for a moment. She then let it all out. "I'm still angry about the circumstances regarding Warners… But I'd be lying to myself if I didn't acknowledge that my feelings for Freddy have heightened. That's why I'm angry. I'm angry at myself."

"Finally. Why is that, though?"

"I don't know, Soph. I'm still trying to figure that out."

Sophie smirked, as if implying something blatantly obvious.

"What is it?" asked Katelyn.

"Forget the current pandemic for a bit. Say Warner calls you tomorrow morning and gives you an offer? Would you accept?"

Katelyn smiled. "I see. The answer is yes, but I want to take him with me."

They laughed.

Katelyn, now relaxed, began to unravel her feelings. "I'm angry that I like a guy like him. He's too nice. But also, so suave. He reminds me of Lloyd. And I hate that. Because I know sooner or later Freddy will also leave me behind in search of that same dream. Fuck, I'm even searching for that dream and look where that's taken me."

"Kate, what if Freddy turns out to be a wimp? You said it yourself, he's too nice. Are you ready to take that gamble?"

Katelyn shook her head, with a smirk on her face. "Since when do we smear on nice guys?" She continued, "I like that about him. And I don't know, he also seems like he's acting like one. I should really get to know him and find out, right?"

Sophie, also with a smile, "Oh, Kate. I think it's time we called an Uber. But yes, my love. Give the boy a call soon."

As they waited for the Uber to arrive, Katelyn said, "This nightmare was telling me I'd be miserable by not telling Freddy how I feel. But also that it's time to move on from the trap that is Venus Trap. Yet, while I'm dying to go, I don't want to leave and leave him behind." She laughed. "What kind of spell is this?"

Sophie turned to her friend and smiled. "Fool's card is full of surprises."

Epilogue

—

An empty space. No bigger than a typical college classroom. One by one, the Bohemians arrived. Freddy was the first one. He sat down on a chair in the middle of the room. Carlos arrived shortly after. He sat next to Freddy.

"Sup, loser," Freddy said. "It's been a while."

They shook hands, like bros.

"Last time we saw each other, was it right after spring break, senior year? How was Rome?" Carlos asked.

"Yeah. It was fun. Charlie ditched us near the end, then came back, and John fell in love with some girl I think, but it was all right."

"John fell in love?" Carlos, said, unconvinced. "*Our* John?"

"Yup," said Freddy, smiling. "Believe me, I'm still trying to figure it out."

A few minutes later Charlie and Blake entered the room. Blake sat next to Carlos. Charlie next to Blake.

"What's with the seat formation?" said Charlie. "I feel like we're in AA."

Blake smirked. "Us? A bunch of alcoholics sitting in a circle? Seems accurate."

They all laughed. Finally, John arrived to the party. He sat next to Blake.

"Okay, which one of you *pendejos'* genius idea was this?" John then looked around the room.

"Our dearest friend, John," said Carlos. "This is an intervention. It seems you have fallen in love? Is this true?"

They all started laughing again.

John just shook his head. "But seriously, though, why the fuck are we all here? And whose seat is this?"

There was still one seat left. No one knew what was going on.

"Alright, since no one is talking I'm just going to leave," said John.

"Wait…" said Blake. He faced the group. "Come on guys, we didn't drive out here for nothing. We are all here, so what's the deal?"

Then, out of the blue, the lights turned off.

"Freddy, is this your doing?" asked Charlie.

"Why are you asking me?"

Then the lights turned back on. The empty seat was

no longer empty. A dark-haired woman, wearing all black, now sat with the Bohemians.

"Hello, boys," the stranger said.

Startled, they almost fell out of their seats.

"How did you just…" Blake's face screamed fear.

"*La bruja…*" said John.

"I'm not a witch, no. I have been called that before, though."

"Whatever, who are you?" said Carlos.

The stranger, her voice radiating confidence, said, "I am the girl of your storybooks. I believe you coined that term, Carlos. I am the architect of your most personal experiences. I've been there since the beginning."

"What kind of bullshit is this?" said Charlie.

"You don't believe me…" said the stranger. "Okay, look at my hair."

The stranger's hair magically switched from black to blonde like a PowerPoint fade-in transition. Then, her face shapeshifted into that of Lucia Visconti. "*Ciao, amico,*" she said to Charlie. She then shapeshifted into Dianna, Brooke, Maddy, Lauren Lancaster, and even James Calhoun. The Bohemians were paralyzed. Their faces of pure "What the fuck."

"I've been manipulating your every move, even without the explicit use of my, let's say, abilities. It's no coincidence that our dear Freddy's first job was at *Venus Trap*. That the statue in Portofino was that of *Aphrodite*…"

"So, I don't have a girlfriend?" said Charlie.

The stranger nodded.

Freddy's eyes opened wide. "So, what happened with Maddy…"

"Yes, Ishtar, queen of Venus, blah blah blah. Your trip through a parallel universe. It happened for real. Didn't I just show you? I was Maddy. Why are you humans so extra?"

"That's definitely something Maddy would say," said Freddy. "Fuck."

"And Dianna," said John. "Lauren too."

"You just expect us to believe this?" Carlos wasn't buying it. "The guys may know all of these names you've mentioned. I'm still here waiting to see when I come into the picture."

"Sally," said the stranger.

Carlos now felt a sudden cold race through his spine. "How do you know that name…"

"I was curious as to why you didn't go on the trip to Rome with the rest of the Bohemians. 'The Bohemians.' Always found that word funny. You didn't go to Rome because you wanted to spend time with her."

"Yes, I made that clear with the boys," said Carlos.

"Bohemians, there's a reason why you are here. There's a reason why I did what I did. Despite what your college textbooks say, us cosmic beings don't just fool around with random humans for the fun of it. I mean, sometimes we do, but not this time."

The stranger now stood up and pointed her finger straight at Carlos. "That right there is not Carlos. At least not the one you spent your college days with. Many years from now I will take Carlos to a remote jungle in Peru. I will traverse deep into his mind with the goal of understanding his love toward Sally. I will succeed and with that knowledge I will manipulate him further. He will forget about her, forever. Instead, he will start loving me."

"This is fucking crazy, man." Blake finally opened his mouth.

"If that's not Carlos, then who is he? And why are you telling us this? Why, why, why everything?!?" Charlie was losing patience.

John chimed in. "Don't tell me Carlos is like the savior of the universe and we need to go back in time or forward in time and stop something from happening so that the future, or the past, or the present, or whatever, can be saved? 'Cause if anyone should be that it's definitely me. I came up with the name 'Bohemians,' for crying out loud."

"No, John Francisco. I've got bigger problems than saving the world," the stranger said with a straight face.

"What is it then?" asked Carlos.

"You... are me."

The boys, still confused, "What???"

"You can fucking shapeshift and you didn't tell us? That's fucked up, Carlos," said Freddy.

"No, he can't," said the stranger. "Look, Bohemians, when I did what I did to Carlos all those years in the future I left a little bit of me behind. I didn't know that would happen. Let's call it a virus. Consequences of my curiosity."

"So, I'm a god?" said Carlos.

"Also no. What you are is *dying*."

Confusion and concern spread across all of their

faces.

"Well, how do we fix it, lady?" said John, pissed.

"You all need to work together. Carlos, you need to fall in love again. As much as you did when you fell for Sally."

"Well shit, that's tough," said Carlos.

"You see, Carlos is what John calls a fuckboy," said Blake.

"I'm sorry. He learned that from me," said John.

"I feel for you, Carlos, but that still doesn't explain why *La Bruja* over here fucked with our hearts," Charlie said, furious.

"It was an experiment. I wanted to see if in the face of love, your hearts would fall. Even John Francisco. If he can change, then so can Carlos."

"Seems easy enough. Carlos, go back to your old ways, boom!" said Freddy. "Better yet, Bruja, why can't you just stop yourself from doing what you did to Carlos in the future. You are a *cosmic being* after all. Your words, not mine. Also, I don't buy a thing you say about Maddy. Bring her the fuck back."

"Unfortunately, it doesn't work like that. Everything that's already happened cannot be changed," said La

Bruja.

"Then what's the point of altering the present if everything is already set in stone?" said John.

"It doesn't hurt to try," said La Bruja.

Carlos, confused, "Wait a minute, you are saying this is just a theory? A god just comes down from the sky, tells me it infected me with certain death, and then says that time cannot be changed, yet has the balls to say that maybe, just *maybe* if I fall in love—which is not an easy thing to do, might I add—that I will magically be cured... Bruja, I want to speak with Jesus."

La Bruja laughed. "In this form I don't have testicles. And after Jesus, do you want Shiva, Ra, maybe Thor? Look, Bohemians, I don't have to help you, but I too, like you, feel guilt. I hate this feeling. I want to make it right. Blake, Charlie, Freddy, John, you've all shown me that there's love in your hearts. I need you to help Carlos find that same spark. That same flame. Maybe then I can make those memories of yours a reality."

"You mean I can see Brooke again?" Charlie said, determined.

La Bruja nodded. "And make you forget me, all of this, as if I never existed. You could see her again, and only her. In fact, she's real. I emulated her out of a Brooke from a parallel universe not too different from this one. Same for Maddy. Just help Carlos not die because of me."

"How would that happen, exactly? Just curious," said Carlos.

"I don't know. All I know is that you'd cease to exist. No one would remember you. Not now, future, or past. Never."

"Well, fuck," they all said.

"How do we even start this?" said John.

"Rome," said Charlie. "Carlos got his cold heart from you and you met Dianna in Rome. If it worked once, it could work again."

"Yeah, I agree," said Blake.

"Me too," said Freddy.

"That sounds like a plan," said La Bruja.

Freddy turned to Carlos, "Well, loser, seems like you are going to Rome after all. It's a matter of life or death."

The Bohemians: Spell of La Bruja is coming soon.

ACKNOWLEDGEMENT

A big thank you to my friend and mentor, Marty Beckerman. For your time, patience, and incredible insights. For making me a better writer.

I promised not to name names, but without her there wouldn't be a page one. Thank you for your love and support. I appreciate you greatly. You know who you are!

And of course, I'm thankful for the boys! The Busby Babes! While the Bohemians are a work of fiction, they wouldn't exist without a source of inspiration. May our hopes and memories live on these fantastical tales and occasional Snapchat callbacks.

ABOUT THE AUTHOR

Carlos has written for AMC Theatres, Phlearn Magazine, among other digital publications on subjects such as film, music, graphic design, and comic books.

He is currently writing a new feature screenplay.

Made in the USA
Monee, IL
22 March 2021